Bossyboots

David Cox

Crown Publishers, Inc.

New York

Once there was a girl called Abigail, who was, so they say, the bossiest girl in all Australia.

I'll tell you the story of the time she caught the stagecoach back home to Narrabri.

First she began by bossing the horses around.

Then she bossed the other passengers.

She even bossed the driver.

As the stagecoach climbed into the hills, the
travelers sat silent. One man kept looking at his fine
gold watch, and a lady fingered her silver brooch.
Little did they know what lay ahead.

For on his lookout up on One-Tree Hill sat Flash
Fred, the wild outlaw. He saw the stagecoach.

Onto his gray mare he bounded. Down the side of
One-Tree Hill he thundered.

He stopped the stagecoach in its tracks.

"All the passengers get down!" Flash Fred yelled, brandishing his gun. And down they got, pale of face and jelly-kneed, and, one by one, handed over...

gold watches, silver brooches, precious stones, purses, and even the food they had brought for the journey.

All went into the outlaw's sack. When he came to Abigail,
Flash Fred said with a leer, "Have you any pennies for me, dear?"

This was just too much to bear. Abigail rose up in her brown-laced boots, raised a finger and exclaimed, "You bossy, bossy man! You ought to be ashamed!"

Flash Fred was left without a word to say.
His face went red. He had met his match.

And so a battle raged across the clearing, back and forth, back and forth, as Flash Fred waved his gun and Abigail shook her finger.

Either could have won, but . . .

Flash Fred tripped and fell.

"All right!" yelled Abigail. "Put down that silly gun right now!"

"Aw heck," said Fred. "It wasn't loaded, anyhow."

So Flash Fred handed back the loot. Onto his old gray mare he clambered, and he headed back up One-Tree Hill, a shamed and broken man.

And as for Abigail . . .

well, she bossed the stagecoach safely home to
Narrabri . . . and it was only half an hour late.